THINGS THAT GO BURP! IN THE NIGHT

by Lynne Moerder

Disney•HYPERION   Los Angeles   New York

Text and illustrations copyright © 2015 by Lynne Moerder
Published by Disney • Hyperion, an imprint of Disney Book Group.
For information
address Disney • Hyperion, 125 West End Avenue, New York, New York 10023.
Printed in Malaysia
First Edition, May 2015
1 3 5 7 9 10 8 6 4 2
H106-9333--5-15015
Library of Congress Cataloging-in-Publication Data
Moerder, Lynne, author, illustrator.
Things that go burp! in the night / Lynne Moerder.—First edition.
pages   cm   Summary: Late at night, brave and hungry mice step out for some treats
and enjoy a feast until an unexpected guest sends them scampering for cover.
ISBN 978-1-4847-1669-4
[1. Stories in rhyme. 2. Mice—Fiction. 3. Food habits—Fiction.] I. Title.
PZ8.3.M7153Thi 2015   [E]—dc23   2014031434
Art is created with digital collage
Reinforced binding
Visit www.DisneyBooks.com

For Mom and Dad and my Tom, with love.

Thanks for the title, Sue.

Thanks for everything, Kevin Lewis

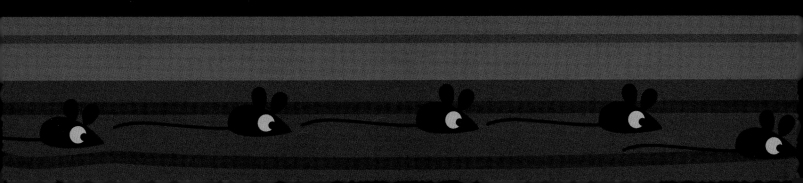

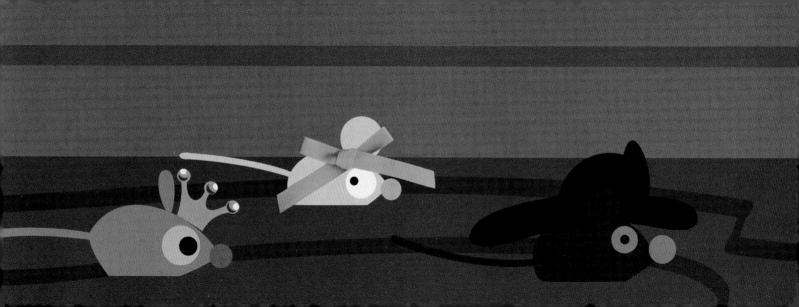

I've heard it said
while you're in bed ...

the mice
step out

to **EAT!**

Hungry mice
in search of treats . . .

FIND > 8 MACARONI

MUNCH

Cheese Queen

find fruits and veggies,

breads and meats —

BERRY BIG!!
7
BLUEBERRIES

Crunchy
cookies!

Sticky jellies!

Grapes and frosting
fill their bellies!

Fresh green peas!

WOW!
4 PEAS

CRUNCH

MUNCH

An olive wrapped
in bacon! TWICE!

Stacks of crackers!

milk to sip
with oatie floaties—

DIVE and DIP!

Turkey Noodle Soup

cheese

ongues go slurp!

2 BANANAS

Big bananas.

And when every mouse
is good and fat . . .

CLATTER!

Scatter!

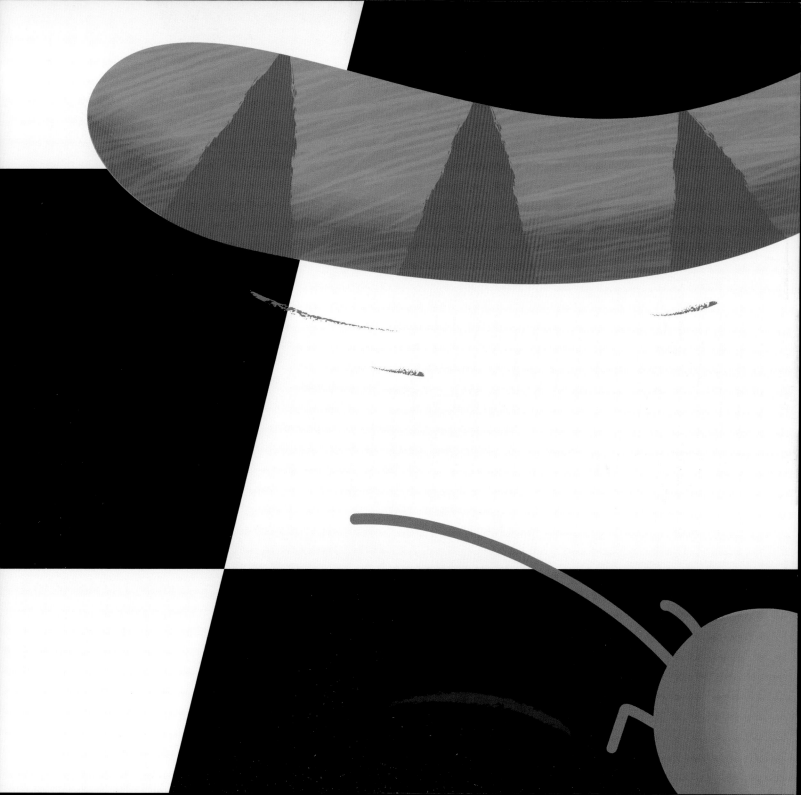

Who woke
the cat?